# Hamster
# MAGiC

# Hamster
# MAGiC

by Lynne Jonell
illustrated by Brandon Dorman

A STEPPING STONE BOOK™
Random House 🏠 New York

To Devin, who reminded me that kids
still believe in magic—L.J.

Many thanks to Julia Hoffner, who lent me her hamster!

Text copyright © 2010 by Lynne Jonell
Illustrations copyright © 2010 by Brandon Dorman

Published in the United States by Random House Children's Books, a division of
Random House, Inc., New York.

Random House and the colophon are registered trademarks and A Stepping Stone
Book and the colophon are trademarks of Random House, Inc.

Visit us on the Web!
www.steppingstonesbooks.com
www.randomhouse.com/kids

Educators and librarians, for a variety of teaching tools, visit us at
www.randomhouse.com/teachers

*Library of Congress Cataloging-in-Publication Data*
Jonell, Lynne.
Hamster magic / by Lynne Jonell ; illustrated by Brandon Dorman. — 1st ed.
p.   cm. — (A Stepping Stone book)
Summary: When the Willows move into a new house, Celia, the youngest of four
children, traps an enchanted hamster, who reluctantly agrees to grant the children
one wish in exchange for his freedom.
ISBN 978-0-375-86660-9 (trade) — ISBN 978-0-375-96660-6 (lib. bdg.) —
ISBN 978-0-375-86616-6 (pbk.) — ISBN 978-0-375-89672-9 (e-book)
[1. Hamsters—Fiction. 2. Magic—Fiction. 3. Moving, Household—Fiction.]
I. Dorman, Brandon, ill. II. Title.
PZ7.J675Ha 2010   [E]—dc22   2009049076

Printed in the United States of America
10 9 8 7 6 5 4 3 2 1

# Contents

CHAPTER I

# Hammy the Third

It all started when the hamster escaped. Everyone thought it was Celia's fault.

"It was *not* my fault," she said. She looked at her big brothers and sister. She opened her blue eyes wide.

"Don't bother to make puppy eyes," said Derek, who was eight and impatient to be nine. "They don't work on us."

"Puppy eyes only work on grown-ups." Tate was almost ten, and pretty, but she didn't like other people to talk about it. She flipped her dark brown ponytail over her shoulder and peered into the empty hamster cage. "How come you left the cage open?"

"I didn't!" said Celia, stamping her foot. "I turned the latch like always, right after I fed him!"

Abner, who was the oldest and felt the burden of this, wiped Celia's eyes. Then he gave her shoulder a gentle shake. "Dry up, will you?"

"And help us look for Hammy," said Derek. "We don't know all the hiding places in this house yet."

But the hamster was nowhere to be found.

"That was our third hamster, too," said Tate, curling up against the dryer like a cat. The four of them were in the laundry room, the last place they had tried. "The parents will never let us get another one."

"They'll blame me," Abner said gloomily.

He drew his knees up to his chin. "They'll say I'm responsible. Or if they don't say it, they'll *think* it."

This was true, he felt, and not only because he was the oldest. He had been named after an elderly relative who had been some kind of hero a very long time ago. A painting of this relative, with a sword, hung in the museum in the city. Ever since Abner had been taken to see it, he had felt that he carried a heavy load.

"You're not responsible. Celia is." Derek kicked at a laundry basket, but it didn't make him feel any better. He scrubbed at his straight, bristly hair and wished he could kick something more satisfying. A football, for instance. But football was best with a bunch of kids— and his friends were far away.

The move had been the hardest on Derek. Just one week ago, the Willow family had left their comfortable old neighborhood, with its houses jammed right up next to each other. Derek had played a last game of street hockey, trying to ignore the men who were loading a moving van in his driveway. And then Mr. Willow honked the horn of the family car, and Derek climbed in and watched through the rear window until they turned a corner and his friends were gone.

"It's only for a year," his parents had said. "And you'll love the house. It's right in the country with lots of room to run around. Woods! A river!" But what Derek wanted most was a block full of kids who might want to toss a football, or shoot baskets, or play a little baseball down at the park.

After a long drive, the moving van had rumbled across a stone bridge. The Willows' car followed it over a narrow river and up a long, winding driveway to the top of a hill. And there was the house, three stories high, with a sprawling front porch and a toolshed and a big old barn, where they parked the car.

A thin belt of woods circled the house. When Derek ran to the edge of the trees and peered down, the few houses he saw were far away. True, the river was nearby. It curved around the base of the hill, and in one place it even widened into a swamp, which looked like fun. But there were no close neighbors at all.

And now there was no hamster.

"I'm telling you, I shut the latch!" Celia blinked three times, hard. She didn't want everyone to think she was turning on the tears.

"We don't really *need* a hamster," said Tate, without conviction. She picked at the ragged edge of her sweatshirt. "Lots of kids go through life without one."

"We need *something* alive," said Abner. "We can't get a good pet—like a dog—until we show we can take care of a little stupid one."

"Hamsters aren't stupid," said Celia. She blinked twice more. "And Hammy the Third was the smartest of all."

"So why did you go and lose him, then?" said Derek.

❦❦❦

Celia was crying at last, but under the stairs, where no one could see her. It was true that she could turn on the tears as needed. But when she was crying for real, she liked to be private.

She really did miss Hammy. Unlike Hammy the First, he did not hide and snuffle under a cloth all day long. And he was not stupid enough to walk off a table when she let him out for a little exercise, like the hapless Hammy the Second. No, Hammy the Third was different.

Maybe it was because they hadn't gotten him from a pet store. They had found him on moving day. He was cowering in the cellar behind a bag of Woofies dog biscuits the previous owner had left behind. A corner had been chewed open and a biscuit pulled out, and Celia thought this was clever of Hammy.

A hamster that had lived on its own just had to be smarter, in Celia's opinion. Hammy the Third was an alert little rodent who always listened carefully when she talked. He had never talked back, but Celia was sure that was only because he was shy.

She had been trying to teach him how to open the door of his cage. She had thought he would be grateful. And if a hamster was grateful, maybe he would say "thank you." And then he would not be shy anymore, and she would have someone to talk to who was littler than she was.

Celia wanted that very much. She was tired of being the baby of the family. But now that Hammy had opened the door of his cage by himself and escaped, she was still the baby— only hamsterless.

Celia stopped crying, hiccupped, and sniffled twice. Her last sniffle seemed more like a
squeak, for some reason. She paused, thinking
about this, and the squeak came again.

It was close. It sounded like Hammy.

Celia felt around in the dark beneath the
stairs, where the suitcases were stacked in a
row. The squeaking was louder now, and she
heard a small bumping noise. She put her ear
next to the small suitcase her mother used for
short trips and listened. It sounded very much
like a tiny voice squeaking "Lemmee out!
Lemmee out! Lemmee out!"

Celia sat back on her heels. Then she went
to find a flashlight.

It took a long time, and she ran into her
mother, who made her pick up some toys she
had left out. Then her father told her to fetch
him some masking tape. Next, Derek caught

her in the hallway and pretended to punch her, and she had to pretend to punch him back or he would say she was soft. But at last she was under the stairs once more, shining the light on the small suitcase.

The bumping had stopped, but from within the case came a faint sound of panting. Celia snapped open the latch and lifted the lid. Inside was a small, golden, slightly sweaty ball of fur.

"What took you so long?" said the hamster. "It's not my fault the lid fell shut!"

Holding the pocket of her pants firmly closed, Celia climbed the stairs to the third floor. This was where the children's bedrooms were, one on either end of a long open space with five windows. Above, wooden rafters held up a high, slanting roof. This room was the best thing about the house, they had all agreed, and it was theirs to set up as they liked. They called it the Loft.

They hadn't finished with it yet, though. Abner was putting together shelves out of bricks and boards, Tate was sorting books to put on the shelves, and Derek was digging in a box of sports gear when Celia came through the door.

"I found the hamster," she said. "And he talks." She pulled Hammy gently from her pocket and held him out with pride.

Tate and Abner glanced at each other. Derek, less careful of her feelings, dropped a hockey stick and snorted.

"He does!" Celia prodded the hamster with her finger. "Say something, Hammy."

The hamster looked annoyed. He lifted his back, twitched his nose, and was silent.

Derek laughed out loud.

Celia lifted the hamster up and stared him right in the eye. "Talk," she said sternly. "You know you can do it."

They were all laughing now, even Abner. Celia ignored them—not an easy task—and whispered in the hamster's tiny ear. "There's no use pretending you can't. You already talked, and I heard you. It's not a secret anymore."

"Give it up, Seal," said Tate, calling Celia by her baby name. "And, Derek, it's not that funny. Stop rolling on the floor. You're full of dust."

Abner hauled Derek up and brushed him off. "You almost had me, Celia. Put him back in the cage, and this time, lock it."

The hamster gave Celia a pleading look.

Celia recognized the hamster version of puppy eyes. "I don't feel one bit sorry for you. Hamsters that won't talk *belong* in a cage."

The hamster snuffled pitifully.

"Besides, I saved your life," Celia pointed out as she tried to stuff the hamster through the cage door. "You probably owe me three wishes or something."

The hamster squirmed in her hand, bracing himself against the wire frame. "Only one!" he squeaked. "One wish only! And it has to be approved by headquarters!"

# CHAPTER 2

# What a Hamster Wants

There was a couch in the Loft. It was big and shabby, and the previous owner had not wanted to move it. But the children didn't mind its drab brown cover with the faded red dots. It was comfortable, and long enough to hold all of them. And it was on this couch they sat as they stared at the small rodent on the floor.

Derek found it easy to believe in a talking hamster. It took a little longer for Tate. And

Abner was still doubtful, some time after it had become clear to the others. But in the end they all understood that they were four very lucky children, for hadn't Hammy mentioned a wish?

"Only it's got to be approved by the Great Hamster," said Hammy, pacing nervous circles on the scarred wooden floor. "And she's not going to like it."

Derek tossed a sofa cushion into the air and caught it neatly. "Who's the Great Hamster?"

"And how do you know she won't like it?" Tate pulled a blanket off the back of the couch and patted it into a soft nest for the hamster. "You don't even know our wish yet."

"*We* don't even know it," added Abner.

"It's not the wish," said Hammy. He stopped his pacing and rubbed his paws over his cheeks, ruffling his golden fur. The white

patch over his eyes gave him a worried look. "She won't like it that I was caught."

"That wasn't your fault," said Celia at once. She got off the couch and knelt beside him.

"Yes, it was," said Hammy miserably. "I wasn't supposed to go near the house. But I couldn't resist those dog biscuits! So crunchy!"

"Hey, I have an idea!" Derek dropped the sofa cushion and leaned forward. "What if you just don't *tell* the Great Hamster? Then you could give us our wish right now."

"Don't tell?" Hammy sat back on his haunches and gave this idea some thought.

"You didn't tell her you were going to our

cellar to eat dog biscuits," Celia pointed out.

"Yes, and look what happened!" Hammy cried. "I got caught!"

"By four very nice children," soothed Tate. "And we would never hurt you."

"But are you going to let me go?" The hamster blinked his brown eyes and sniffled twice.

The children glanced at the empty hamster cage. It sat on a packing crate near the window. The late-afternoon sun shone between the metal bars of the cage and laid a crisscross pattern along the floor.

"Um—" said Celia.

Derek wouldn't meet Hammy's eyes. He took a tennis ball out of his pocket and began to pick at the lint.

"Of course we *want* to let you go," said Tate carefully. She twined the end of her ponytail around her finger.

"We can't, though." Abner bent over the golden hamster with a worried look. "We'll get in trouble."

Hammy squeaked in alarm, looking past him.

"No, really, we will," said Abner.

"Will what?"

All eyes turned to the doorway of the play-room, where Mother stood.

"Uh . . . ," said Abner.

"Will take care of our hamster," said Tate, who could think on her feet. She scooped up Hammy from the blanket, scraped his clinging paws from her fingers, tucked him gently into the open cage, and shut the door.

"I hope so," said Mrs. Willow, smiling. "I'm afraid you have been rather hard on hamsters so far."

In the cage, Hammy reared back, looking suddenly distressed.

Abner stood up. "We'll take good care of *this* one, though."

"We promise," said Tate.

Derek and Celia nodded eagerly.

"Good," said Mother. "But you shouldn't let him out anymore. Hamsters are fast, you know. They can run and hide and trap themselves in very dangerous places."

"We didn't take him out," Celia said. "He undid the latch all by himself."

Mother fished in her pocket and came up with a safety pin. "He won't be able to undo this," she said as she fastened the door to the wire cage. "Now take my advice and keep your hamster safe in the cage."

The children looked at one another.

"What about when we clean the cage?" asked Tate. "Can't we take Hammy out then?"

"Yes, of course, but be very careful not to

let him go. If you want a bigger pet one day, you'll have to show you can take care of a smaller one."

Abner sighed.

Mother gave his shoulder a pat. "Don't forget to get washed up, all of you. Supper is in twenty minutes."

The door shut behind her. Hammy pressed his furry face against the wire mesh of the cage. He looked at them meltingly from his big brown eyes.

"I can't take this," said Abner. He turned his back on the hamster and stalked out to the bathroom across the hall. The others heard the splash of water as he washed his hands.

Derek grabbed his hockey stick and began pushing the tennis ball back and forth along the floor, not looking at Hammy. "How can we keep him locked up? He talks and everything."

Chewing on the end of her ponytail, Tate curled up on the couch again. "I know. It's like putting one of us in jail."

Celia crouched next to the cage and tried not to cry. She wasn't going to do it twice in one day, no matter what. But when Abner came back, she clutched at his arm. "Please, Abbie. We *have* to let him go."

"Oh, I suppose," said Abner bitterly. "I might as well say goodbye to ever getting a dog, though."

Tate shrugged. "Look on the bright side, Abs. At least we get a wish first."

"And if you set me free," said Hammy, "I *will* let you have your wish right now. I don't think we need to bother the Great Hamster . . . and you probably don't want to go all the way to the river and get your feet all sandy. . . ."

"So what *are* we going to wish?" Derek flipped

22

the blade of his hockey stick, and the tennis ball hit the wall with a *thwack*. "I wish—"

"Don't say it!" ordered Abner. "Don't say the words 'I wish' until we've all agreed. Right, Hammy?"

"That would be best," said the hamster. "Just to avoid any accidents."

Derek shrugged. "Okay, then, let's just tell our ideas. I say a swimming pool."

"With a twisty slide!" said Celia, clapping her hands.

"How about horses?" Tate bounced on the couch, making the springs creak. "One for each of us!"

"I *could* wish for a dog," said Abner. "If Mom and Dad would let us keep it."

"I'd rather have a motorbike," said Derek. He picked up the tennis ball and tossed it from hand to hand. "Or all my friends here for a visit— Hey!" He sat up straight. "Why don't we say we want to go home? Back to our old neighborhood!"

Abner frowned. "I guess we could. The people living in our house now are only renters. Mom and Dad could tell them they had to go."

"But what about Dad?" Tate laced her fingers together around her knees. "He's doing important work for the university this year. That's why we moved in the first place. And what about Mom? She's taking the year to paint."

The children were silent. They didn't want to ruin their father's work, and their mother had been wanting to paint pictures for a long time. And now, with a year off from her other job, she could.

The sun, lower in the sky, streamed through the windows and lit the rafters of the big, shabby Loft, turning them orange. Abner put his elbows on the sill of an open window and stuck his head through.

"This isn't such a bad place, Derek," he said. "We can have a lot of fun here."

The others came to stand beside him. They looked out at the rosy sky, down at the trees that circled the house, and past the trees to the river, glinting like a golden thread in the last rays from the sun. The stone bridge arched above the water like something from a fairy tale, and all the children remembered at once that they hadn't yet run down to see it.

Derek slumped. "Okay," he said. "I guess we could just get motorbikes, then."

Hammy rattled the bars of his cage to get their attention. "You don't understand," he said unhappily. "I can't give you motorbikes or anything like that. You have to make a *hamster* wish."

The children turned from the window to stare at him.

"So what is a hamster wish?" asked Tate.

Hammy sat back and picked lint from between his toes. "Something a hamster would want, of course."

Tate knelt on the floor and began to paw through the books she had sorted.

"We have to wish for something a *hamster* would want?" repeated Derek. He stopped tossing the tennis ball. It fell from his hands and rolled to the middle of the floor.

"Well, if that's not good enough for you," said Hammy stiffly, "then you don't have to wish for anything at all."

"We didn't say that," said Abner, "but—"

"I found it!" Tate held up a small volume. *"How to Care for Your Hamster,"* she read aloud.

The others looked at her blankly.

"Don't you see? This will tell us everything that hamsters want!"

Abner and Celia moved to either side of Tate, and all three huddled over the pages. "'Hamsters like seeds,'" Tate read. "'They like unsalted nuts and chew toys. They love to gnaw—'"

"I don't want to give up a dog for chew toys," said Abner. He ran his finger down the page. "Let's see. They love to climb. They're desert animals and don't like to get wet—"

"There goes the swimming pool," muttered Derek from behind them. "Celia, move over, will you?" He gave her a little shove.

"But I want to see," protested Celia.

"You can't even read," said Derek, edging in beside Tate.

"I can, too!" Celia cried.

"Just baby books." Derek bent over the book. "Hey, it says some hamsters like to sit in their food dishes!"

Everyone laughed except for Celia, who was mad at Derek and feeling sorry for herself. She saw Hammy's wounded look and went to stand by his cage. She felt sorry for him, too.

"Look at what else they like to eat!" Derek pointed to a picture. "Worms! Beetles! That's gross!"

"It's not gross to *Hammy*," said Celia. She reached out a finger to the paw that Hammy had poked through the bars. "And he likes dog biscuits, too."

Hammy looked at her gratefully. "Woofies," he whispered. "They're the best."

His tiny hamster paw gripped her finger. It tickled, and Celia tried not to laugh. She didn't want Hammy to think she was making fun of him.

"Wait, I've got it!" Derek rolled back on the floor, snickering. "Let's wish for a hamster wheel! We could take *turns*!"

"Stop it!" cried Celia. "You're hurting his feelings!"

No one seemed to hear.

" 'Hamsters like to burrow in wood shavings,' " Tate read aloud, " 'and hay.' "

"I remember our old hamsters doing that," said Derek, sitting up. "But I never knew why."

"I think it's because—" began Celia.

"It's because they dig in the wild," said Abner. He moved his finger along a line of text. " 'Hamsters create tunnel systems, with separate spaces for food, sleeping, baby hamsters—' "

"Tunnels might be good," said Derek.

Celia was tired of being ignored just because

she was the smallest. And, looking at Hammy, she knew he felt the same way. "I know something a hamster wants," she said suddenly. "Hammy's tired of being little, and I am, too. I want to be big."

Derek eyed her with scorn. "That's not a hamster wish. Why would a hamster want to be big?"

"Some hamsters might," said Celia stubbornly. "And I *do* want to be big! I wish I was bigger than *you!*"

Hammy blinked. "You *wish*? Okay, then," he said. He blew out his cheeks and shut his eyes. His toes curled. His ears went flat.

And Celia began to feel very strange indeed.

CHAPTER 3

# What a Hamster Needs

There was a *swoosh* in the room, and a swirling of grit like blowing desert sand, and the children shut their eyes. When they opened them again, Celia *had* become big.

She had also become a hamster.

She was a pretty big hamster—about the size of a large dog—and her fur was pale, with gray markings. She had a pink nose, small alert ears, and startled blue eyes.

There was a moment of shocked silence.

"My sister's a hamster," said Abner in a tone of disbelief.

"Tunnels would have been better," Derek said. "Why did you make such a dumb wish, Seal?"

"I didn't want to be a big hamster!" Celia wailed. "I wanted to be a big *girl*!"

"Yeah, well, no hamster would wish for *that*," Derek pointed out.

Tate tipped her head to one side. "She's kind of cute. And she still looks like Celia, sort of."

Strangely enough, she did still look like Celia. Blue eyes, pale fur—and a paw in her mouth.

"Honestly," said Tate, "stop sucking your thumb, Celia—I mean, paw. I thought you broke that habit."

Celia hastily took her paw out of her mouth. "I just wanted to see if it tasted different."

"But what are we going to do now?" Abner turned to the others. "I mean—she's a *hamster*.

I don't mind it myself," he added hurriedly as the tears stood in Celia's blue hamster eyes. "But the parents aren't going to like it at all."

Tate leaned over the cage. "Hammy, why did you do that? You're going to have to take it back. And you must have known it wasn't our real wish. . . . Stop snuffling, Celia," Tate added crossly. "You wanted to be big, so now you should act like it."

Hammy stood up on his hind legs and squeaked.

Abner rolled his eyes. "Give it up, already. We know you can talk."

"No, I think he's trying," said Tate. "Look at him!"

Hammy's mouth was working, and his paws were waving, but nothing came out but squeaks.

"You used up all his magic," said Derek. "Nice going."

"Tunnels would have used just as much," Celia answered hotly, her fur ruffling.

"But what are we going to do?" Abner muttered, and then swung sharply on his heel. "What's that?"

Footsteps sounded in the hall. There was a knock on the door. "Suppertime!" called their father.

The four children—rather, three children and a hamster—looked at one another in panic as the doorknob turned.

Tate snatched the blanket and flung it over Celia. "Snuffle!" she hissed.

"*Now* you want me to snuffle?" Celia whispered.

Father poked his head in. "Are you coming?" He paused. "What's Celia doing under the blanket?"

"She's playing hamster," said Tate, prodding Celia with her foot. "And we were wondering . . ."

Celia began to make snuffling noises, and the blanket moved from side to side.

Tate moved toward her father. "Would it be

all right if we had supper up here in the play-room, on trays? We'd carry everything," she added quickly.

Celia's snuffles and squeaks became louder. Tate shot a look at Abner, who thumped the blanket-covered mound and hissed something under his breath. Celia fell silent.

Tate laid a hand on her father's arm. "We hurt Celia's feelings," she said, speaking low. "So she pretended to be a hamster instead of our sister. And then we thought if we went along with it, and let her eat hamster food off a tray, she might feel better. We really do feel bad."

She gave Derek a sharp glance, and he arranged his face in a look of sorrow.

Father raised an eyebrow. "That's very nice of you kids. I'll see what I can work out with your mother."

"And maybe," said Tate brightly, "you and

Mom could have a nice dinner alone, for a change! With candles!"

Father grinned. "Come on down, then, all of you. You can get your trays."

"But not Celia," Tate reminded him. "Because she's a hamster, of course."

"Of course," said Father.

Abner caught at Tate's sleeve as Father left the room. "How do you do that?" he whispered. "Think on your feet like that, so fast?"

Tate shrugged. "I don't know. I just do."

"Well, it's a very useful skill," said Abner with feeling as he followed her down the stairs.

☙ ☙ ◎

Mother had sent up a bowl of fruit with supper, as extra hamster food, and Celia was entertaining Derek by stuffing her cheek pouches with apples.

"Can you fit in two bananas?" asked Derek with deep interest.

"Mmph woom," said Celia.

Abner eyed Celia's bulging cheeks with gloom. "We are in deep, deep trouble." He had finished his supper, but he had not enjoyed it.

"I know," said Tate. "And Hammy still isn't talking."

Celia was having a great deal of fun being a hamster, and she didn't plan to worry until she had to. She spit out the apples and grinned at Derek with her long hamster teeth. "What's for dessert?"

Derek lifted the lid of a square pan and whooped. "Chocolate cake!"

"You can't have any, Celia," said Tate. "Chocolate is poison for hamsters. I read it in the book."

"No fair!" cried Celia.

"Can I have her piece?" asked Derek.

Celia humped her shoulders and rested her nose on her chest. She felt strangely unsatisfied. She wasn't exactly hungry anymore, but she had a powerful urge to chew something—something hard, like *wood*. . . .

"Hey! Stop that!" Abner dragged her away from the sofa leg. "Look at those teeth marks!"

Tate picked up the hamster book again. "She

can't help it. Hamsters need to gnaw. It keeps their teeth from getting too long."

Celia had found something new to chew.

"No! Not my hockey stick!" Derek's cry was anguished.

Celia looked up guiltily.

"Oh, let her have it," said Abner. "It's wrecked now, anyway, and it'll keep her happy while we think of what to do next."

"It won't keep *me* happy," said Derek miserably, watching as his beloved hockey stick began to look like a chew toy.

Tate patted him on the shoulder. "It's for a good cause."

"All right," Abner went on, "let's figure this out. Hammy said something about a Great Hamster."

Tate nodded. "She was supposed to approve any wishes."

"We should have listened," whimpered Derek.

"Too late now." Abner gazed at the small hamster in the cage. "I think we should try to find this Great Hamster and see if she can help. If she has the power to approve wishes, maybe she can do something to take them back."

"But we don't know where she lives." Tate bent over the book again. "It says here that

hamsters are really good runners. They'll run as much as five miles for something to eat!"

"Really?" Derek looked at Celia with new respect.

"So think about it. The Great Hamster could be really far away."

"But she's not," said Derek. "She's— Whoa!"

Celia had dropped the hockey stick to do acrobatics on the couch. She scampered up the arm to the back and flipped off, tumbling into Derek before rolling away. Her claws clicked across the wood floor in a rapid tattoo. She raced the length of the playroom and skidded into the boys' bedroom at the far end.

"Wow," said Derek.

Celia came dashing back again, a pale, fuzzy streak darting past in a bundle of fur and paws. She disappeared into the girls' bedroom on the other side, and there was a faint crash.

In his cage, Hammy was racing, too, but on his hamster wheel. The dry squeal of metal going round and round mixed with Celia's panting as she came lolloping back.

"Sorry!" she gasped. "It was just the lamp." And she was gone again, circling the room like a dust mop gone mad.

"Kids? Are you done with those trays yet?" Mr. Willow called from the stairway.

"Coming, Dad!" Tate rattled the plates convincingly. She added to Abner under her breath, "You've got to stop her!"

Abner snatched up the blanket and shoved one end in Derek's hands. Together, they advanced on Celia. She was madly leaping, trying to see how high she could climb up the wall.

"What's all that noise?" Father's feet sounded on the steps.

"Oh—they're all playing hamster," called Tate. She stacked the trays and staggered to the door with her arms full. Behind her, the room echoed with thumps and squeaks and muffled grunts, but she didn't dare look back.

The door opened inward, catching her elbow and sending the trays flying. Plates and silverware and cups and bits of uneaten food fell with a clatter to the floor. Father made sure that Tate was all right, then helped to pick up the mess.

When he at last looked up, Abner and Derek were sitting on the couch, breathing hard, with a blanket-wrapped bundle between them.

"Playing hamster seems like a very energetic game," Father observed. "Celia, are you all right?"

Abner nudged the bundle.

"I'm fine, Dad!" Celia's voice, while slightly muffled, was clearly happy. "I'm having lots of fun!"

"You're being true to nature, anyway," said Father. He glanced at the hamster cage, where the wheel was still going round. "Hamsters do seem to get very active in the evening. And all through the night, of course."

Abner's face held a look of doom. "Hamsters stay up *all night*?"

Father grinned. "Well, yes. They're nocturnal. But *you* four hamsters are going to have to go to bed soon, I'm afraid."

When Father had gone away with the dishes, Abner let Celia out of the blanket on the condition that she stay perfectly still. And just to make sure, two pairs of hands held her firmly in place.

"No more running," said Abner sternly. "No more crashing into things."

"And no more climbing the walls," added Tate, petting her sister between the ears to calm her.

Celia looked from one to the other. "I can't help it," she said. "It's like something comes over me, and I just have to *move*."

"I feel the same way when I play sports," said Derek. He picked up the hamster book and paged through it. "Hamsters really do need a lot of exercise. Too bad we *don't* have a giant hamster wheel."

Celia was wriggling again. She slipped from under Abner's and Tate's hands and popped up on the couch, panting. "You can't make me stay still all night," she begged. "Please let me run? I'll be very, very quiet."

Abner shook his head. "Mom and Dad's room is right under ours. They'll hear you, for sure."

Celia kicked her short hind legs, banging them against the couch. "You don't know how it feels!" she cried in a passion. "I'm a hamster! I was born to run!"

"I'd like to see her run bases," said Derek. "She *is* fast. Couldn't we take her outside?"

"Oh, yes!" Celia clasped her paws together. "Please? Please please pleeeeeeeease?"

"We could take her out after the parents are asleep, maybe," said Tate, stroking Celia's back.

"And we were going to look for the Great Hamster, anyway," added Derek.

"But we don't know where she is," said Abner. He leaned over Hammy's cage, where the little hamster was still racing in his wheel. "*You* could find the Great Hamster, couldn't you?"

Hammy threw a startled glance at Abner's looming face, jumped off the wheel, and dove into a pile of wood shavings in the corner. He burrowed until there was nothing to be seen of him but one furry golden ear.

"I get the feeling he doesn't want to," said Tate. "I bet he thinks he's going to get in trouble."

Abner stared at the hamster's quivering ear. "He deserves it," he said. "And he didn't even tell us where the Great Hamster lives so we could find her ourselves."

"Yes, he did," said Derek. "Don't you

remember? When he told us he wouldn't bother her about our wish. He said her burrow was almost to the river, and if we went we would get our feet all sandy."

Abner looked at the oversized, slightly sweaty hamster that was Celia and thought things over. He wasn't a boy who liked to sneak around behind his parents' backs, and he didn't like doing things that could get him into trouble. But he couldn't let his sister stay a hamster forever.

"All right," he said. "As soon as we're sure Mom and Dad are asleep, we'll go to the river-bank and look for the Great Hamster."

# CHAPTER 4

# The Great Hamster Speaks

Of course, the children had to get into their pajamas and say good night to their parents. Celia, who usually liked to be tucked in and kissed good night, called out from the girls' room that hamsters did *not* want kisses and hugs.

Mother said, "I hope you're not still a hamster tomorrow, because I'd like to see my little girl again," and Celia felt a sudden longing for her mother so strong that she almost jumped out of bed and ran to her. Abner had a pang somewhere in his chest—what would his mother say if Celia never *was* a little girl again?—and he felt more responsible than ever.

But Tate said, "I'm sure she'll be your girl again in the morning," which she felt was a nice thing to say, even if she didn't quite believe it.

Derek didn't say anything. He was already fast asleep in the boys' bedroom, sprawled across the bed with the covers in a bunch. Then after a while Tate went to sleep, too, and it was up to Abner to stay awake. He had to keep Celia quiet and listen for the silence that meant his parents had finally gone to bed.

It was dark and very late when Abner lifted a trembling Hammy from the cage. "Listen," he said, "we're going to find the Great Hamster, and you're going to help us."

Hammy looked up from Abner's hand, blinking nervously.

"And no pretending you don't know where she is, just so you don't get into trouble," Abner added.

Hammy wiped his paws over his nose and looked as if he were about to cry.

"I'll tell her that you didn't mean to hurt anybody," said Abner, and he tucked Hammy gently in his pocket.

Three sleepy children and one very large hamster tiptoed down the stairs. Celia's nails click-clacked on the wooden steps, so Abner picked her up. She was not too heavy to carry if he rested now and then. In the dark, Abner could almost pretend that Celia was a little girl again, dressed in very fuzzy pajamas.

But she wasn't, of course. And when they got to the front door, Celia turned her head, sniffing.

"What's that wonderful *smell*?" She wriggled from his arms and slipped to the floor.

Abner reached out, but before he could grab her, Celia had dashed between his legs and down the cellar steps. By the time he caught up with her, she was in the corner with the bag of Woofies dog biscuits, stuffing her cheek pouches full.

"Come *on*!" said Abner. "Don't be a pig."

"But they're so *yummy*, Abner!" Celia said thickly, through falling crumbs. "I can't explain it, but this is the best thing I've eaten in my life!"

From Abner's pocket, Hammy squeaked agreement.

"So chewy!" Celia closed her eyes in bliss. "Yet so crunchy!"

Hammy squeaked again, a sharp series of chirps.

"Okay." Celia snagged two more doggy treats with her small, four-fingered paw and tucked them in Abner's pocket with Hammy. She looked up at her brother, her whiskers quivering. "You should try one, Abner. They're so sweet! So tasty! So—"

"I get the idea," Abner said grumpily. "But let's go." He got a good grip on the scruff of her neck and urged her up the stairs.

The night air was cool, and the sky was flecked with stars. High above rode the moon, and the three children looked about them with wonder. They had never been out so late before.

But Celia was a hamster, and she wasted no time in looking at the stars. She darted across the yard and into darkness.

"Hey!" Abner's whisper was hoarse. He took off after his reckless sister—and then he tripped. Luckily, he remembered to twist so that he fell on the side where Hammy wasn't. The little hamster was only shaken, not squashed.

Abner had landed heavily on his shoulder and wrenched it, and twisted his knee. He lay on the ground, his pajamas getting damp from the grass, and wished most passionately that he weren't the oldest. If he were the youngest, he could throw a tantrum and refuse to go one more step, and no one would think anything of it.

"What do we do now?" asked Tate. She took Hammy from Abner and soothed him, petting the fur between his ears with a careful finger.

Abner struggled to sit up. What should they do now? It wasn't much good going to see the Great Hamster without Celia. "I think," he said slowly, "that we should—"

"Hey!" Derek scrambled to his feet. "Look!"

In the moonlight, Derek's pointing finger could be clearly seen. Abner looked, and saw a black shadow rapidly coming near. It panted like an energetic dog.

"Everybody grab her when she comes by," Abner said, his voice low. He got into position, his sore shoulder forgotten. Celia galloped past, pale in the moonlight like some kind of furry ghost. But when Abner leaped, his knee gave way under him, and he missed her by inches.

Tate hadn't moved at all. "Don't look at *me*," she said. "I'm holding Hammy."

Abner was too busy nursing his knee to answer. Still, when a sliding, grunting sound came to his ears, he looked up. There was the shadow of Celia again, only she was moving much more slowly. And dragging behind her, hanging grimly on to one hind leg, was Derek.

"Good man, Derek," said Abner. "Celia, stop this minute and let him get on your back. No, I don't care if you think he's heavy. You need something to slow you down."

They all went on toward the river. Derek's weight kept Celia to a walk, and he was happy to ride. "You're my horse," he said, gripping the loose skin behind her ears. "And I'm going to call you White Streak."

"I'm a *wild* horse," said Celia, and she began to buck.

"Settle down," snapped Abner. His shoulder hurt, his knee was making him limp, and he was in no mood for any nonsense.

They walked on in silence. The only sounds were the whisper of their feet on grass and the buzzing of night insects. Stars twinkled around the edge of the sky, where the moon was not so bright, and the air was cool and magical.

When they came to the tall row of cypress trees that marked the edge of the road, they followed them down a slight incline to the river, which chuckled and murmured in between sandy banks.

"Now," said Abner, "does anyone have any string?"

No one did. "Why do you need it?" asked Tate.

Abner shrugged, wincing as his shoulder moved. "How were you going to get Hammy to lead us to the Great Hamster once we got here?"

Tate frowned. "I don't know. I guess just put him on the ground and tell him to go find her."

"Not good enough," Abner said. "What if he decided to run away? No, we've got to use some kind of leash."

"But he's a *person*," said Celia, her whiskers bristling. "He talks. You can't just treat him like a *pet*."

"He doesn't talk anymore," said Abner. "And we still need a leash."

Tate, after a moment's thought, pulled the ribbon from her ponytail and held it out to Abner. "Is this good enough?"

Abner examined the long, thin ribbon. It was soft yet strong. "Perfect." He tied a loose knot in one end and threaded the other end through the hole in the middle. Then he slipped the loop over Hammy's head.

"Now," Abner said, "this won't hurt you. It'll just make sure we don't lose you in the dark. But don't try to run away, or you might get choked."

Hammy at once headed up the bank, away from the river's edge.

"Oh, no you don't," said Abner firmly, lifting the hamster back down. "No trying to avoid it. You said she lived by the river, and we would get our feet sandy, and here we are. She's got to be close. So just stay on the sand and head for her burrow, and we'll call her."

Softly, one after the other, the children called, "Great Hamster! Great Hamster!" And though Abner felt half-foolish, and Tate a quarter so, they went on calling, and kept Hammy from climbing the banks in his attempts to escape. Derek called, too, but Celia wouldn't. She paced along the top of the low bluff above the sandy bank, because something about the water made her feel very uncomfortable.

At last, tired out, Abner stopped. He sat down on a fallen log, and everyone else dropped where they stood. Tate cupped Hammy in her hands. "Why won't you lead us there? You know where she lives."

Hammy, looking desperate, squeaked.

"I'm sorry you can't talk anymore," Tate went on, "but really, Hammy, you can do better than this."

"He's just a coward," said Abner bitterly. "He's scared of the Great Hamster, so he keeps trying to run away."

The little hamster squeaked again and again. Celia, above them on the bank, stopped her pacing and listened. Then she squeaked back.

Hammy, after one startled moment, erupted in a flurry of shrill chirps. He waved his paws and stamped his hind feet in Tate's palm.

Celia looked down at her brothers and sister. "He's been trying to lead you all along. The Great Hamster does live near the river, but she's not right *next* to it. Hamsters hate water."

"The book did say that hamsters were desert animals," said Tate thoughtfully.

"Celia!" Derek scrambled up the bank, grinding sand into the knees of his pajamas. "Can you speak Hamster now?"

Celia hesitated. "I don't know," she said. "I can't really tell what the words are. It's more like I just know what all the squeaking *means*."

"Well, we'd better do what Celia says." Tate climbed the bluff and set Hammy on the ground once more. "Okay, Hammy, go."

Abner followed unhappily. If Hammy was just pretending, they would never find the Great Hamster. But if Hammy had been trying to lead them to her all along, then Abner had made a big mistake, and been mean to Hammy as well. Neither option made him feel good, and his knee hurt most abominably.

They were in sand still, only it wasn't right by the river. They kicked through soft, sculpted dunes on the raised land of the upper banks. Scrubby grasses poked out of the sand, and here and there was a tree with twisted roots that showed above ground.

"Hey, I didn't know this was here!" Abner said, looking around at the dunes with interest. "What a cool place to play!"

"Hammy knew it was here," said Tate, and Abner felt ashamed. And then, suddenly, he felt even worse, for a shadow rose out of a hole in the ground. It cast a longer shadow before it, from the moon at its back.

It was a hamster, larger than average (though not nearly so large as Celia). It stood on its hind legs and folded its paws across its furry chest. "Who," it said, raising its voice strongly, "has put a leash on my child?"

## CHAPTER 5

# Magic Beneath

"Who has put a leash on my Forvten?" demanded the Great Hamster again, her voice stern and terrible.

The children looked at one another blankly. *Forvten?*

"You mean Hammy?" said Derek.

The Great Hamster's fur stood out straight, and she seemed to increase in size. "Forv-ten," she repeated, leaning on each syllable, and her long front teeth gleamed in the moonlight. "He is the fourth child of my tenth litter. Four-of-ten. Forvten for short, and certainly not *Hammy*, whatever you may think."

"Oh," said Derek.

"He never said he minded being called Hammy," said Celia from behind the others.

The Great Hamster seemed to notice the very large hamster for the first time. She reared back and studied Celia, looking her up and down. "I don't know you," the Great Hamster said at last. "Are you from Hollowstone, or do you come from Away?"

For the second time the children exchanged glances, and Tate asked the obvious question. "What is Hollowstone?"

"Not 'what,'" snapped the Great Hamster. "'Where.' Right *here* is Hollowstone, and burrowers who live here are not ordinary anima—" She bit off the word and puffed out her cheeks.

"I don't want to answer your questions until you answer mine."

Abner felt himself flush. "It's my fault. I put the leash on Ham—er, Forvten. And I'm not sure where Hollowstone is, exactly, but we live in the house on the hill." He bent down, feeling both guilty and annoyed, and fumbled with the knotted ribbon around Hammy's neck.

Released, the small hamster squeaked, and squeaked again. He scampered to his mother and leaned his head against her side.

The Great Hamster patted his back and listened as he squeaked some more. Then she looked up. "I see," she said. "You made a very foolish wish, a wish that was almost too big for Forvten. He granted it and drained his power. And now you think I can do something about it."

"Can't you?" begged Abner.

"Please?" added Tate.

The Great Hamster pulled at her whiskers, frowning. "No. You'll just have to wait until it wears off."

"But it will wear off, then?" Abner took some hope from this. "When?"

"I don't have any idea," said the Great Hamster. "We burrowers don't make the magic. We just let it soak in. Once it's used, it has to build up again." She looked down at her small and shamefaced son. "It will be awhile before Forvten can even speak again, I'm afraid. But with any luck"—here she gave him a fond little shake—"he might have learned his lesson."

"Ham—Forvten didn't mean to hurt anyone," said Abner, remembering that he had promised to say this.

The Great Hamster put her paws on her

hips. "He knew the rules. Get all wishes approved first. He should have told you that."

"He did," said Tate miserably. "But we
didn't listen."

"I was the one who made the wish," said

Celia. She flattened out her furry body on the sand. "So it's really my fault."

"If it hadn't been Celia," said Derek suddenly, "it would have been me. I was going to wish for tunnels. Lots of them."

The Great Hamster's stern, whiskered face softened. "Well, at least you stand up for each other, as litter-mates should."

Derek looked uncomfortable. "Sometimes," he said.

The Great Hamster smiled, her cheeks bunching, and waddled over to the nearest tree. She climbed up the exposed roots to a perch the height of Derek's shoulder, and settled herself with the dignity of a queen on a throne, or a storyteller.

There was an awkward silence.

"What now?" whispered Tate. "Should we just go home?"

Abner shook his head. "I don't want to give up," he whispered back. "Not while Celia is still a hamster."

Celia crept closer. "I don't mind it," she said. "Not really. And I like giving Derek rides."

Derek threw an arm over Celia's round, fuzzy back. "When my hockey stick is all chewed up, I'll let you have my bat," he promised.

Tate yawned. "Maybe everything will be all right in the morning. Can't we just go home and go to bed? I'm so tired."

"Me too," said Derek, catching Tate's yawn.

"I should be sleepy," said Celia, bouncing on her paws, "but I'm not. Can I run, Abner?"

Abner smothered his own yawn and nodded. "Go ahead, but stay close, and come back when you get tired. Come on, the rest of you. I want to ask the Great Hamster a few questions."

The roots of the giant cottonwood rose high out of the sand and sheltered a hollow place beneath. Derek lay flat on his back, facing the summer night's sky, and Tate curled up in the sand, her head pillowed on a wide, low root. Abner leaned against the smooth wood—the roots were surprisingly comfortable—and looked up at the Great Hamster, who sat a few inches above his head.

He cleared his throat. "So how does the magic build up? And what do you mean, you let it soak in?"

The Great Hamster shrugged her furry shoulders. "Who knows how it happens? I just know it comes from beneath."

Abner scooped up a handful of sand and let it sift through his fingers. "The magic is below ground?"

The Great Hamster nodded. "It might be from the earth, or stone, or water, or something else. But the more time an animal spends underground, the more magic it soaks up."

"So that's why you said it was *burrowers* who weren't ordinary animals."

"And only burrowers *in* Hollowstone Hill. From the river to the road, and the road to the forest."

"That means our house is smack in the

middle," said Abner slowly. He toyed with the idea that came to him. There would be other small animals near the house, easily caught, who might grant wishes, too. Maybe it wasn't too late to wish for a dog. If two or three burrowers wished together, it wouldn't be too much for any one of them.

"Why do you call it *Hollowstone* Hill?" asked Tate sleepily.

The Great Hamster chuckled. "You humans and your questions. It's called Hollowstone because that's what it's always been called. Who knows why? Who cares?"

Celia came zipping past, a flash of teeth and moonlight-tipped fur. Behind her ran a number of smaller shadows. "We're playing tag!" cried Celia. "I'm faster than anybody!"

Abner looked after her thoughtfully. "Listen," he said, "I can see why you wouldn't want to use up your own magic to wish Celia was a girl again."

"Certainly not," said the Great Hamster. "I need all my magic to manage these burrowers and keep them from more dumb-fool mistakes like the one Forvten, here, made."

Abner glanced at Forvten, formerly known as Hammy. He was curled up on a knot of wood and snoring lightly.

"But what if," Abner began, "it wasn't just *you* wishing? What if you got a lot of the bur-rowers together, and they all used just a little of their magic? Could they turn Celia back again?"

The Great Hamster looked at him shrewdly. "And what makes you think I'd want to do that?"

The question hung in the air. Abner looked to Tate for help, but her eyes were closed.

Derek, flat on the sand next to her, was breathing deeply.

"Just to be nice?" Abner suggested.

The Great Hamster chuckled. "Not good enough. Find me something I want, young man, and I'll consider it. You humans," she said again, tapping her claws against the hard tree root. "It's always 'What can the rodent do for me?' and never 'What can I do for the rodent?' You dig up our burrows. You interfere with our lives. And you half killed my son with your silly wish!"

"We didn't mean to." Abner jammed his hands in his pockets. He nervously rolled lint and crumbs between his fingers—and then he stopped. "I know something you might want," he said slowly.

The Great Hamster sniffed. "I doubt it."

Abner brought his hand out of his pocket.

In his palm was a half-chewed dog biscuit.

The Great Hamster's nose quivered. She slid down the tree root to the ground.

Abner held out his hand. "Try it," he coaxed. "Just take a *little* taste."

"It looks like a piece of wet cardboard." The Great Hamster closed her eyes, swaying a little. "But it smells—"

"Delicious?" suggested Abner. He moved his hand a little closer. "Scrumptious? Too yummy to resist?"

The hamster leaned forward and took a small nibble.

"Oh, *my*." Her paws fluttered before her furry chest, and she gazed at the dog biscuit in awe.

"It's Woofies," said Abner. "The very best kind."

There was a sound like a strangled bark as the Great Hamster lunged forward. Soft, fuzzy jowls pressed against Abner's fingers as she mouthed the doggy treat and settled down to a blissful crunching.

"I can get you some more," said Abner.

The hamster swallowed, licked her whiskers, and looked up. "More?"

Abner turned his head. An excited babble

of squeaking voices grew louder, and Celia appeared again, surrounded by leaping small rodents. They were mostly chipmunks and gophers, as far as Abner could see, and they seemed upset.

"Listen!" Celia held up her paws. "Of course I always win. I'm the fastest—what do you expect?"

An eruption of squeaks filled the air.

"I can't help it if I'm the biggest!" Celia reared back, her whiskers quivering.

More squeaks. Much waving of paws.

Celia listened, her head lowered. "Oh, all right. Let's play something different, then. How about capture-the-acorn? You can have more on your team. . . ."

They moved off, their shrill voices fading. Abner turned back to the Great Hamster, who was licking her paws to get the last tiny crumbs.

"I know where there are lots more dog biscuits," Abner said. "And I can bring them tonight, *if* you turn my sister back."

"Oh . . . oh, dear . . ." The Great Hamster's delicate paws combed her cheek fur and scrubbed her ears. "I don't know if it will work. I just don't know. It's not really a hamster wish, to turn into a human—not usually, anyway. I'm sure the rest of the burrowers feel the same. But perhaps all together . . ."

"Just try it," urged Abner. "I'll bring the whole bag of Woofies if you promise to try your best."

The Great Hamster tapped her claws together. "Very well. But if it works, I want you to promise me something, too."

"What?"

The Great Hamster leaned forward and whispered in his ear.

Abner looked at her for a moment. It was not a promise he wanted to make.

"Okay," he said, sighing.

"And what about those others?" The Great Hamster nodded at Tate and Derek, still fast asleep on the sand. "Can you speak for them, too?"

"Yes." Abner looked at his sister and brother. They would agree. And if they didn't, he'd just have to make them understand.

"All right, then." The Great Hamster scampered down from the tree root and onto Abner's knee. "Let them sleep. It will take me most of the night to gather the burrowers. And in the meantime—"

Abner nodded. "I'll get the Woofies."

# CHAPTER 6

## Out of Time

The burrowers stood lined up in rows, small to large. Rabbits and woodchucks were at the back. Gophers, hamsters, and chipmunks came next. And the tiny moles and meadow mice were in front. They looked soberly at Celia, lying asleep in a fat, furry bunch among the tree roots, and then at her brothers and sister watching anxiously from the sidelines. Abner clutched the bag of Woofies and held the chewed corner shut.

"Ready?" said the Great Hamster, raising her paws like a conductor. "And—begin!"

The burrowers screwed up their eyes and flattened their ears. Paws tightened and whiskers trembled.

But Celia stayed a hamster.

"Up one more notch!" called the Great Hamster, and the burrowers tried even harder. Cheeks puffed out and hind feet thumped.

"There!" Tate pointed. "Is something changing?"

"I don't see it," said Derek after a pause.

"It's only the light," said Abner heavily. He looked to the east, where the sun was just lifting above the trees, and his shoulders slumped. His parents would be getting up soon, and Celia was still a hamster.

"I don't dare tell them to increase the magic," said the Great Hamster. "It's almost too much even now."

"The rabbits do look a little faint," said Tate.

"Maybe it takes a while to have an effect?" suggested the Great Hamster. "I don't really know. We've never tried to reverse a wish like this before."

Abner nodded, but without hope. They had run out of time. He tucked the bag of Woofies dog biscuits among the tree roots and backed away. "We've got to get home," he said. "Thank you for trying."

But Celia proved impossible to wake up. She lay in a soft, fuzzy heap, her head pillowed on her paws and her sides moving in and out with her breath.

"She was awake enough last night," said Derek. "She never stopped running."

"That's why she's so tired now," Tate said. "Hamsters stay up at night and sleep during the day. But Celia was a girl yesterday, not a hamster, and so she didn't sleep then, either."

"We'll have to carry her." Abner said this with a sigh, for he was tired, too. He'd been awake all night, and hurt his shoulder and twisted his knee. But what was weighing him down most of all was the problem of how to tell their parents about Celia.

Their path back was all uphill. Stumbling, dirty, and still in their pajamas, the three children worked their way slowly through the dunes and up the road, carrying Celia between them. She was pudgy, with short little legs, and hard to get a grip on. More than once she almost slipped.

They stopped over and over again to get a firmer hold, and staggered on. "Almost—there," gasped Tate as they neared their front door. "Just a few—more feet."

But they had forgotten about the stairs. Inside, they looked up the long flight of steps to the second-floor landing, and knew there was another flight beyond that.

They had decided to try to keep Celia a secret for one more day. Abner didn't really believe that they would find a way to change her back. But he wanted to put off explanations for just a little while longer. He was too tired to face it all right now.

Bumping, slipping, grabbing for the banister,

they dragged the dead weight of Celia up to the
second-floor landing, but there they dropped to
the floor.

"I can't," whispered Tate, almost crying. "Not one more step."

Derek, collapsed in a heap, moaned in agreement.

Abner slumped against the wall, catching his breath. Down the hall, behind their parents' bedroom door, there was a noise of bedsprings and then a shuffling of feet.

The sound gave the children a last spurt of energy. "We'll roll her," Abner said, low and urgent. The three got on their knees and began to push the big hamster up, step by step.

Halfway, the energy left them as suddenly as it had come. Derek had hardly pushed past the second step anyway, and Tate had petered out, too. Abner turned and braced himself against the limp and sleeping hamster, who seemed to grow heavier every moment. "Come on," he said hoarsely. "Help me—I can't hold her up alone."

Feet jammed against wall and banister, Derek, Tate, and Abner pressed their backs against Celia's warm, soft body to keep her from falling. They were in shadow, and it was possible that their parents might head straight to the kitchen for their coffee and never look up.

And at first it seemed that it might happen. Father headed straight downstairs, fumbling for the light switch and missing it. But Mother's slippers made a gritty noise on the landing, and she looked down at the floor, and then up.

"What on earth?" Still in her robe, she stared up at her children. "How in the world did you get so filthy? Just look at your pajamas! And there's sand all over the landing!"

Abner looked at the others. Faces smudged, pajamas torn, and with twigs in their hair,

Derek and Tate looked as if they had spent the night outside. Which they had.

The three children gazed silently down at their mother. There didn't seem to be anything useful to say.

"We went out," said Abner at last. He waited hopelessly for her to discover that her youngest child was a hamster of unusual size.

"Is that Celia behind you? Don't tell me you took her outside in her pajamas, too?" Mother swept up the stairs and stopped in front of the children. "Move aside, you three. I'll speak to you later."

Wordlessly, Abner, Tate, and Derek moved. Their mother gasped.

"She's even filthier than the rest of you!" Bending down, Mother lifted Celia in her arms and stamped up the stairs. "I suppose I should be grateful that she's still in her play clothes

from yesterday, but does this mean that she never put on pajamas at all? Into the tub with you, one after the other. And you'll put on clean clothes and sweep up all the sand before any of you have breakfast!"

The three children stood looking up at Celia, who hung over her mother's shoulder—blond-haired, blue-eyed, fully human, and as dirty as they had ever seen her.

"She changed!" cried Tate. "You changed, Celia!"

Derek whooped. "The Great Hamster was right—it just took time!"

Abner thumped up the stairs behind Mother, in unbelieving joy. He took hold of Celia's hand, which dangled over her mother's arm—skin, not fur! It was real!—and gave it a shake.

Celia smiled at her big brother. "Don't be mad, Mom," she said. "They took good care of me. And I had a *lot* of fun playing hamster."

# CHAPTER 7

# Lucky Willows

The children were busy all morning.

They swept up the sand and suffered their scolding. They took baths, one after the other. And they even did extra chores, to show they were sorry. So after lunch, Mrs. Willow said that they had done enough and could play.

But all they wanted to do was sleep.

"Let's take a nap," said Tate when Mother had gone.

Derek put his head down on the table. "I vote we nap right here."

"I'm not *that* sleepy," said Celia.

"Easy for you to say," mumbled Derek. "You slept the whole time we carried you."

Abner yawned so widely, his eyes watered. "We'd better go to our rooms so the parents won't see us sleeping. They would wonder what we had been doing all night."

"That would be hard to explain," Tate said. She pulled Derek to his feet and herded him up the stairs.

But when they got to the third floor, they did not go straight to their beds. Instead, they stood at the window, looking out. Over the large and scrubby yard, past the line of trees, they could see the gleam of the river. Near it was a curving, pale line that might have been the top of a sand dune.

"We'll have to keep the promise I made, now," said Abner.

Tate nodded. "The burrowers *did* turn Celia back into a girl again. It's the least we can do."

"It's too bad, though," said Derek wistfully. "I wanted to make a wish for myself."

"What did you promise?" asked Celia. She had been sleeping for that part.

Abner breathed on a smudged pane of glass and polished it with his shirttail. "We all promised—that means you, too, Celia—never to ask another burrower for a wish."

"Never?" Celia asked. "Not even a little wish?"

Abner shook his head. "We're just lucky it all turned out the way it did." His eyes strayed to the empty hamster cage. They would never get a dog now, for their parents thought they had lost another hamster. But still, Abner felt lucky.

Derek gazed out the window. "With all

that magic coming up from the ground, though, don't you think there might be more out there, on Hollowstone Hill?"

"Maybe," said Tate.

"I hope so," said Celia.

"I wonder what kind?" said Abner.

The End

# About the Author

Lynne Jonell is the author of the popular *Emmy and the Incredible Shrinking Rat,* a *Booklist* Editors' Choice and one of *School Library Journal*'s Best Books of the Year, as well as *The Secret of Zoom* and seven picture books. Although she doesn't really care for rats, hamsters, or any kind of rodent at all, she still keeps writing about them. Please don't ask her why. She doesn't understand it herself.